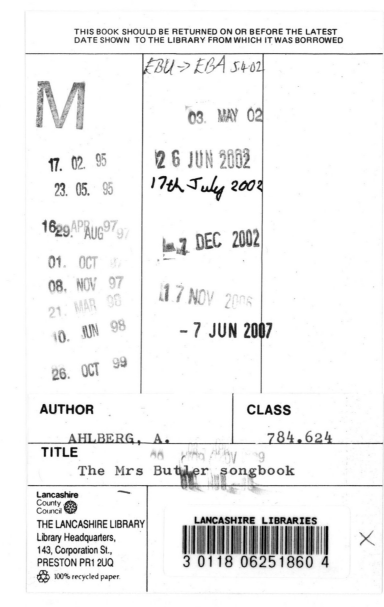

THE MRS BUTLER SONGBOOK

Allan Ahlberg and Colin Matthews

THE MRS BUTLER SONGBOOK

ARRANGED BY GAVIN BRYARS

ILLUSTRATED BY FRITZ WEGNER

VIKING

VIKING

Published by the Penguin Group
Penguin Books Ltd, 27 Wrights Lane, London w8 5tz, England
Penguin Books USA Inc., 375 Hudson Street, New York, New York 10014, USA
Penguin Books Australia Ltd, Ringwood, Victoria, Australia
Penguin Books Canada Ltd, 10 Alcorn Avenue, Toronto, Ontario, Canada m4v 3b2
Penguin Books (NZ) Ltd, 182–190 Wairau Road, Auckland 10, New Zealand

Penguin Books Ltd, Registered Offices: Harmondsworth, Middlesex, England

First published 1992
10 9 8 7 6 5 4 3 2 1

Text copyright © Allan Ahlberg, 1992
Illustrations copyright © Fritz Wegner, 1992
Music copyright © Colin Matthews, 1992
Musical arrangements copyright © Gavin Bryars, 1992

The moral right of the author and illustrator has been asserted

'Everybody Was a Baby Once' first appeared in the play *The Giant's Baby*
by Allan Ahlberg produced and performed by Polka Children's Theatre.

Consultant Designer: Douglas Martin

Set in 12pt Aldus by Rowland Phototypesetting Ltd,
Bury St Edmunds, Suffolk

Printed in Great Britain by William Clowes Ltd, Beccles and London

A CIP catalogue record for this book is available from the British Library

ISBN 0-670-83235-9

Teacher's prayer

Let the children in our care
Clean their shoes and comb their hair;
Come to school on time – and neat
Blow their noses, wipe their feet.
Let them, Lord, **not** eat in class
Or rush into the hall en masse.
Let them show some self-control;
Let them slow down; let them **stroll**!

Let the children in our charge
Not be violent or large;
Not be sick on the school-trip bus,
Not be cleverer than us;
Not be unwashed, loud or mad,
(With a six-foot mother or a seven-foot dad).
Let them, please, say 'drew' not 'drawed';
Let them know the **answers**, Lord!

Contents

For All Singers and Players

The songs in this book are settings of poems from Allan Ahlberg's highly popular books, *Please Mrs Butler*, and *Heard it in the Playground*, plus four entirely new pieces: 'Night School', 'A Happy School', 'Scatterbrain' and 'Everybody was a Baby Once'. Colin Matthews' music is tuneful and lively, but also playable and singable – you don't need brilliant musicians to perform it. The songs can be used in a variety of situations and can also, of course, be acted. You feel like entertaining somebody? Then simply choose your songs, mix in a few related jokes and sketches, invite your audience – and put on the show in the hall!

A few technical points: piano parts have been kept as simple as possible and the vocal range is rarely demanding. There are guitar chords in all of the songs. There are parts for recorders (although voices humming or singing "ah" could be substituted) and some suggestions for percussion. There's scope, too, for experimenting – try using various shakers or tuned percussion, for example, in the Latin American style pieces such as 'Is That Your Apple?' and 'Excuses' and a cabasa for 'Emma Hackett's Newsbook'. More able pianists can also experiment with the piano parts. For example, in 'Scissors' the piano solo can be replaced with a rock 'n' roll style improvisation. The songs are as versatile as you make them. Happy singing!

Part One  **PLEASE MRS BUTLER**

1 Complaint

1. The teachers all sit in the staffroom.
   The teachers all drink tea.
   The teachers all smoke cigarettes
   As cosy as can be.

2. We have to go out at playtime
   Unless we bring a note
   Or it's tipping down with rain
   Or we haven't got a coat.

3. We have to go out at playtime
   Whether we like it or not.
   And freeze to death if it's freezing
   And boil to death if it's hot.

4. The teachers can sit in the staffroom
   And have a cosy chat.
   We have to go out at playtime;
   Where's the fairness in *that*?

2 Emma Hackett's Newsbook

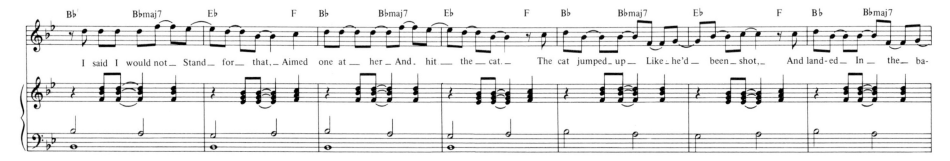

* *optional harmony*

1. Last night my mum
   Got really mad,
   Wo, wo, wo!
   And threw a jam tart
   At my dad.
   No, no, no!
   Dad lost his temper
   Then with mother,
   Threw one at her
   And hit my brother.

2. My brother thought
   It was my sister,
   La, la, la!
   Threw two at her
   But somehow missed her.
   Ha, ha, ha!
   My sister,
   She is only three,
   Hurled four at him
   And one at me.

3. I said I would not
   Stand for that,
   Wow, wow, wow!
   Aimed one at her
   And hit the cat.
   Miaow, miaow, miaow!
   The cat jumped up
   Like he'd been shot,
   And landed
   In the baby's cot.

4. The baby –
   Quietly sucking his thumb –
   Ga, ga, ga!
   Then started howling
   For my mum.
   Wa, wa, wa!
   At which my mum
   Got really mad,
   And threw a Swiss roll
   At my dad.

5. Dad lost his temper
   Then with mother,
   Threw one at her
   And hit my brother.
   My brother thought
   It was my sister,
   Threw two at her
   But somehow missed her.
   My sister,
   She is only three,
   Hurled four at him
   And one at me.
   I said I would not
   Stand for that,
   Aimed one at her
   And hit the cat.
   The cat jumped up
   Like he'd been shot,
   And landed
   In the baby's cot.
   The baby –
   Quietly sucking his thumb –
   Then started howling
   For my mum.
   At which my mum
   Got really mad . . .

   Oh, oh, oh!
   Oh, oh, oh!
   Oh, oh, oh!
   OH!

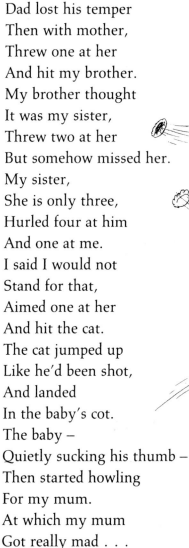

3 Scissors

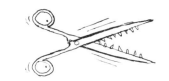

Boogie woogie tempo

1. No - bo-dy leave the room.___ Ev - ery-one listen to me.___ We had___ ten pairs of scissors At half - past _ two,___ And

now there's on - ly three.___ 2. Se - ven _ pairs of sci - ssors___ Dis-app - eared_ from sight. Not one of you leaves Till we find them. We can

stop here all _ night! ___ 3. Sci-ssors don't.lose them-selves,___ Melt a - way___ or ex - plode.___ Sci-ssors have not _ got _ Legs _ of their own_ To go

1. Nobody leave the room.
    Everyone listen to me.
    We had ten pairs of scissors
    At half-past two,
    And now there's only three.

2. Seven pairs of scissors
    Disappeared from sight.
    Not one of you leaves
    Till we find them.
    We can stop here all night!

3. Scissors don't lose themselves,
    Melt away or explode.
    Scissors have not got
    Legs of their own
    To go running off up the road.

4. We really need those scissors,
    That's what makes me mad.
    If it was seven pairs
    Of children we had lost,
    It wouldn't be so bad.

5. I don't want to hear excuses.
    Don't anybody speak.
    Just ransack this room
    Till we find them,
    Or we'll . . . stop here all week!

4 *The School Nurse*

Bouncy, not too fast

1. We're lin - ing up to see the nurse And in my o - pin-ion there's no - thing worse. It

is the thing I al - ways dread. Sup - po - sing I've got *nits* in my head. 2. I go in - side and

sit on the chair, And she ruf-fles her fin - gers in my hair. I feel my face get-ting hot and red. Sup - po - sing she finds *nits* in my head.

RECORDER

3. It's ta-king a-ges; it must be bad. Oh, how shall I tell my mum and dad? I'd ra-ther see the den-tist in-stead Than be the one with

nits in his head.　　　　　　　　　4. Then she taps my arm and says, 'Next please!' And I'm out in the cor-ri-dor's cool-ing breeze.　　Yet

still I can feel that sense of dread.　　Sup-po-sing she had _____ found nits in my head.

1. We're lining up to see the nurse
   And in my opinion there's nothing worse.
   It is the thing I always dread.
   Supposing I've got *nits* in my head.

2. I go inside and sit on the chair,
   And she ruffles her fingers in my hair.
   I feel my face getting hot and red.
   Supposing she finds *nits* in my head.

3. It's taking ages; it must be bad.
   Oh, how shall I tell my mum and dad?
   I'd rather see the dentist instead
   Than be the one with *nits* in his head.

4. Then she taps my arm and says, 'Next please!'
   And I'm out in the corridor's cooling breeze.
   Yet still I can feel that sense of dread.
   Supposing she *had* found nits in my head.

5 Picking Teams

Slowly

mp 1. When ___ we pick teams in the play - ground, What -

(Intro.)

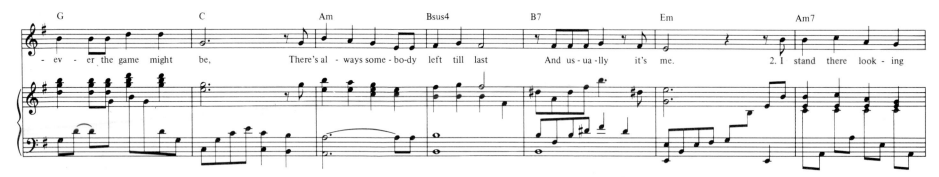

- ev - er the game might be, There's al - ways some - bo - dy left till last And us - ua -lly it's me. 2. I stand there look - ing

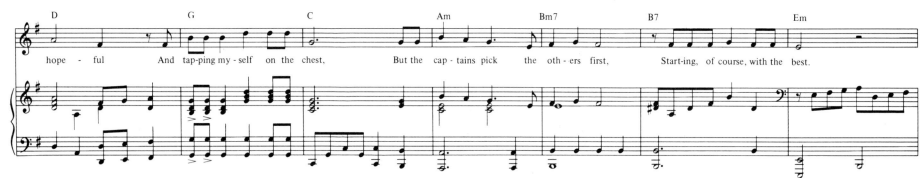

hope - ful And tap - ping my - self on the chest, But the cap - tains pick the oth - ers first, Start - ing, of course, with the best.

* lower voice part optional addition

1. When we pick teams in the playground,
    Whatever the game might be,
    There's always somebody left till last
    And usually it's me.

2. I stand there looking hopeful
    And tapping myself on the chest,
    But the captains pick the others first,
    Starting, of course, with the best.

3. Maybe if teams were sometimes picked
    Starting with the worst,
    Once in his life a boy like me
    Could end up being first!

6 Colin

Brightly

f 1. When you frown at me like _ that, Co - lin, _ And wave your arm in _ the _ air, _____ I

know just what _ you're go - ing to say: _ 'Please, Sir, it is - n't _ fair!' _ 2. It is - n't fair On the foot-ball _ field If their team scores a _ goal. _

It is - n't fair In a crick-et _ match _ Un - less you bat *and* _ bowl. 3. When you scowl at me that _ way, Co - lin, _ And mut - ter and slam _ your _ chair, _____ I

pic-ture the words _ on the grave-stone_ now. They'll say: IT IS NOT FAIR. _____

molto rit.

1. When you frown at me like that, Colin,
   And wave your arm in the air,
   I know just what you're going to say:
   'Please, Sir, it isn't fair!'

2. It isn't fair
   On the football field
   If their team scores a goal.
   It isn't fair
   In a cricket match
   Unless you bat *and* bowl.

3. When you scowl at me that way, Colin,
   And mutter and slam your chair,
   I always know what's coming next:
   'Please, Sir, it isn't fair!'

4. It isn't fair
   When I give you a job.
   It isn't fair when I don't.
   If I keep you in
   It isn't fair.
   If you're told to go out, you won't.

5. When heads bow low in assembly
   And the whole school's saying a prayer,
   I can guess what's on your mind, Colin:
   'Our Father . . . it isn't fair!'

6. It wasn't fair
   In the Infants.
   It isn't fair now.
   It won't be fair
   At the Comprehensive
   (For first years, anyhow).

7. And when your life reaches its end,
   Colin,
   Though I doubt if I'll be there,
   I can picture the words on the
   gravestone now.
   They'll say: IT IS NOT FAIR.

please, Sir,
it isn't fair!

7 Our Mother

on our___ shoes,___ When we were told not to go in the park, Be - cause it would be get - ting dark.
on our___ thumbs,___ And in our beds the ti - ni-est crumbs From the cakes we said we had not eaten.

Our

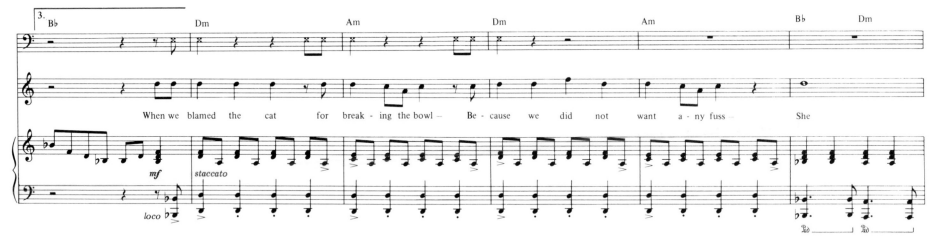

3.

When we blamed the cat for break - ing the bowl — Be - cause we did not want a - ny fuss — She

knew it was us. Our mo - ther is a de - tec-tive. She's a great find - er of clues.

1. Our mother is a detective.
   She's a great finder of clues.
   Our mother is a detective.
   She's a great finder of clues.
   She found the mud on our shoes,
   When we were told not to go in the park,
   Because it would be getting dark.

2. Our mother is a detective.
   She's a great finder of clues.
   Our mother is a detective.
   She's a great finder of clues.
   She found the jam on our thumbs,
   And in our beds the tiniest crumbs
   From the cakes we said we had not eaten.

3. Our mother is a detective.
   She's a great finder of clues.
   Our mother is a detective.
   She's a great finder of clues.
   When we blamed the cat for breaking the bowl –
   Because we did not want any fuss –
   She *knew* it was us.

   Our mother is a detective.
   She's a great finder of clues.

8 *I Did a Bad Thing Once*

I did a bad thing once.
I did a bad thing once.
I took some money from my mother's purse.
I took some money from my mother's purse.
I took the money for bubble gum.
I took the money for bubble gum.
What made it worse, she had bought me some.
What made it worse, she had bought me some.
She'd bought me some for being good.
She'd bought me some for being good.
While I'd been vice versa,
So to speak – that made it worser.

9 When I was Young

1. When I was young and had no sense, I used to lie in a crib. I used to sle - ep for hours and hours And drib - ble on my bib. And

(v. 2 & 3)

drib - ble on my bib. And drib - ble on my bib. I used to sleep for hours and hours And drib - ble on my bib. _____

1. When I was young and had no sense,
   I used to lie in a crib.
   I used to sleep for hours and hours
   And dribble on my bib.
   And dribble on my bib.
   And dribble on my bib.
   I used to sleep for hours and hours
   And dribble on my bib.

2. I had no sense when I was young.
   I sat in a high chair.
   I spooned my dinner from the plate
   And threw it everywhere.
   And threw it everywhere.
   And threw it everywhere.
   I spooned my dinner from the plate
   And threw it everywhere.

3. I could not talk when I was young.
   I could not catch a ball.
   I only sucked the books I had,
   I did not read at all.
   I did not read at all.
   I did not read at all.
   I only sucked the books I had,
   I did not read at all.

4. When I was young and had no sense,
   I used to lie in a crib.
   I used to sleep for hours and hours
   And dribble on my bib.

10 Lost

3. Al - so, his swim - ming towel has gone Out of his P. E. bag, he says, and one Of his

socks, as well, which is pur -ple and green With a darn in the heel. His sis - ter Jean 4. Has a pair ve - ry si - mi - lar. And while I re-mem-ber, is there news of those Fair Isle

Gloves which Ray - mond lost that time Af - ter vi - is - ting the pan - to - mime? 5. Well, I think that's all. _____ I ____ will close now, Yours sin -

1. Dear Mrs Butler, this is just a note
   About our Raymond's coat
   Which he came home without last night,
   So I thought I'd better write.

2. He was minus his scarf as well, I regret
   To say; and his grandmother is most upset
   As she knitted it and it's pure
   Wool. You'll appreciate her feelings, I'm sure.

3. Also, his swimming towel has gone
   Out of his P.E. bag, he says, and one
   Of his socks, as well, which is purple and green
   With a darn in the heel. His sister Jean

4. Has a pair very similar. And while
   I remember, is there news of those Fair Isle
   Gloves which Raymond lost that time
   After visiting the pantomime?

5. Well, I think that's all. I will close now,
   Yours sincerely, Maureen Howe.
   P.S. I did write once before
   About the hat that Raymond wore

6. In the school play and later could not find,
   But I got no reply. Still, never mind,
   Raymond tells me now he might have lost the note,
   Or left it in the pocket of his coat.

11 *Bedtime*

1. When I go upstairs to bed,
   I usually give a loud cough.
   This is to scare The Monster off.

2. When I come up to my room,
   I usually slam the door right back.
   This is to squash The Man in Black.

3. Nor do I walk to the bed,
   But usually run and jump instead.
   This is to stop The Hand –
   Which is under there all right –
   From grabbing my ankles.

I us - ual-ly slam the door right __ back. This is __ to squash The Man in Black. __

3. Nor do I walk to the __ bed, But us- ual-ly run __ and __ jump. in - stead. __ This is __ to stop The Hand — Which is un - der there all __ right — From

grab - bing my an - kles. _____

12 *School is Great*

f 4. Foot – ball leaves me with the stitch, But I'd miss my play - time to mark the pitch. 5. Cook-ing a cake gives

cresc. *f*

you a thrill, But clean-ing the bowl out is bet - ter still.

mp

6. Sto - ry's nice at the end of the day, But I'd ra - ther emp - ty the rub-bish a - way. 7. Yes, school is great – though I'll tell you what:

ff

Go - ing-home - time beats the lot!

1. When I'm at home, I just can't wait
   To get to school – I think it's great!

2. Assemblies I could do without,
   But I love it, giving the hymn-books out.

3. Writing's fun, when you try each letter,
   But sharpening the pencils first – that's better!

4. Football leaves me with the stitch,
   But I'd miss my playtime to mark the pitch.

5. Cooking a cake gives you a thrill,
   But cleaning the bowl out is better still.

6. Story's nice at the end of the day,
   But I'd rather empty the rubbish away.

7. Yes, school is great – though I'll tell you what:
   Going-home-time beats the lot!

13 Swops

I'll give you
A penny chew
A plastic whistle
Pot of glue
A suck of sherbet
Small canoe
A piece of string

A cockatoo
A bag of crisps
And a kangaroo!
For your Milky Way.
What do you say?

No!

What do you say? _____   No! *(shout)*

14 Is That Your Apple?

Lively, not too fast, syncopated

1. Is that your ap - ple?_What a charm-ing sight!_You_know I'd be your best_ friend.For a lit-tle bite.   You could come to my house._You_ could cud-dle my cat._ E - ven
(v. 2)

Is that your apple?

1. Is that your apple?
   What a charming sight!
   You know I'd be your best friend
   For a little bite.
   You could come to my house.
   You could cuddle my cat.
   Even dig in my sand-pit,
   If you fancy that.

2. Is that your apple?
   What a charming sight!
   You know I'd be your best friend
   For a little bite.
   You could come to my house.
   You could stay for your tea.
   Even play with my train-set,
   It's all right with me.

3. Is that your apple?
   What a charming sight!
   You know I'd be your best friend
   For a little bite.
   You could come to my house.
   You could come like a shot.
   We could . . . Oh, you greedy pig,
   You've gone and eaten the lot!

15 Only Snow

Smoothly

1. Out - side, the sky _____ was al - most brown, The

clouds were hang - ing low. _____ Then all of _ a sud - den _ it hap - pened: _____ The

GLOCKENSPIEL

air was full of snow. _____ 2. The child - ren rushed to the

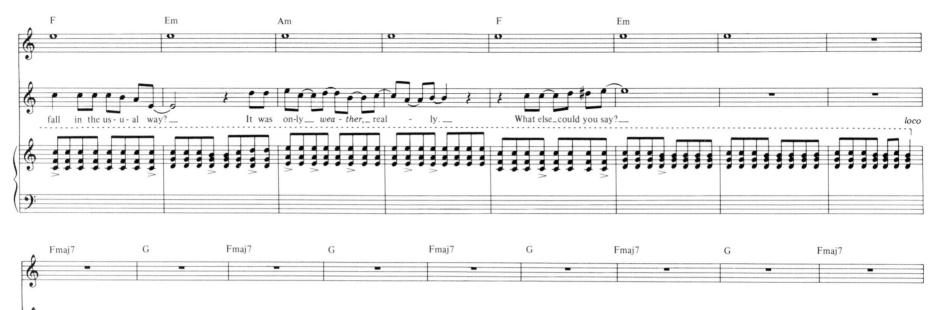

fall in the us-u-al way?_ It was on-ly _ wea-ther,_ real — ly. _ What else_could you say?_

loco

5. The teach — er sat at _ her desk _ Put - ting

GLOCK.

ticks _ in a row, _ While_the child - ren stared through _ the steam — y glass At the on — ly

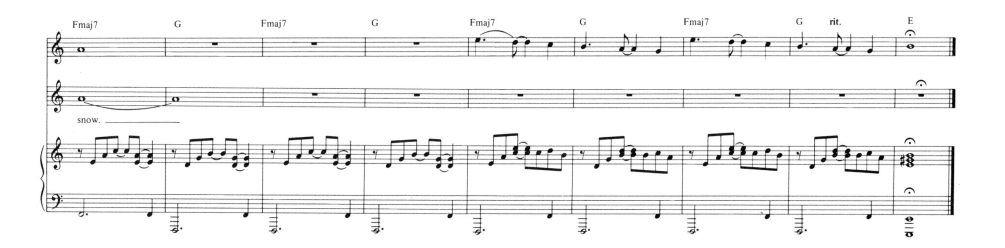

1. Outside, the sky was almost brown,
   The clouds were hanging low.
   Then all of a sudden it happened:
   The air was full of snow.

2. The children rushed to the windows.
   The teacher let them go,
   Though she teased them for their
   foolishness.
   After all, it was only snow.

3. It was only snow that was falling
   Out of the sky,
   Only on to the turning earth
   Before the blink of an eye.

4. What else could it do from up there
   But fall in the usual way?
   It was only *weather*, really.
   What else could you say?

5. The teacher sat at her desk
   Putting ticks in a row,
   While the children stared through the
   steamy glass
   At the only snow.

16 Eating in Class

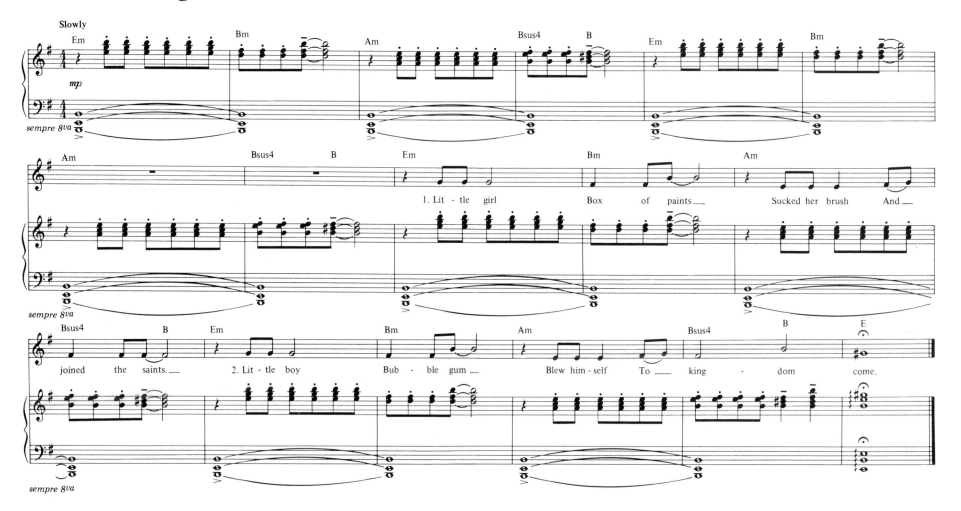

1. Little girl
   Box of paints
   Sucked her brush
   And joined the saints.

2. Little boy
   Bubble gum
   Blew himself
   To kingdom come.

17 Reading Test

right   pic-ture   think   sum - mer   pe-o . . .   pop-ple . . .   peep . . .

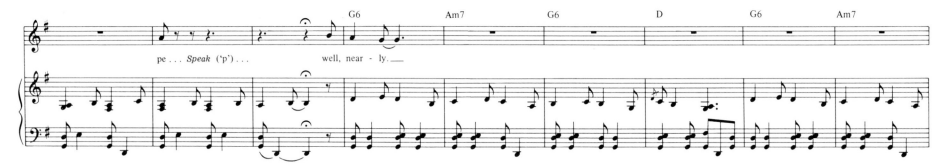

pe . . . *Speak* ('p') . . .   well, near - ly. ____

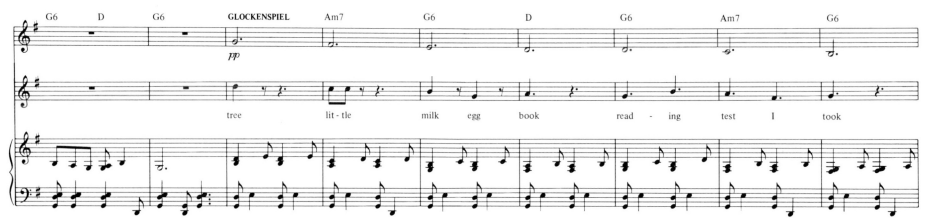

tree   lit - tle   milk   egg   book   read - ing   test   I   took

school   sit   frog   play - ing   bun   it   was   not   much   fun.

tree	little	milk	egg	book
read	ing	test	I	took
school	sit	frog	playing	bun
it	was	not	much	fun
flower	road	clock	train	light
still	I	got	it	right
picture	think	summer	peo . . .	

popple . . .

peep . . .

pe . . .

p . . . well, nearly.

tree	little	milk	egg	book
read	ing	test	I	took
school	sit	frog	playing	bun
it	was	not	much	fun.

18 Excuses

Tempo 'La Bamba'

1. I, I, I've writ on the wrong page, Miss. My pen-cil went all blunt. My book was up-side-down, Miss. My book was back to front. My book was back to front. My book was up-side-down. My pen-cil went all blunt. Oh, oh, oh! 2. My mar-gin's gone all crook-ed, Miss.

1. I, I, I've writ on the wrong page, Miss.
   My pencil went all blunt.
   My book was upside-down, Miss.
   My book was back to front.
   My book was back to front.
   My book was upside-down.
   My pencil went all blunt.
   Oh, oh, oh!

2. My margin's gone all crooked, Miss.
   I've smudged mine with my scarf.
   I've rubbed a hole in the paper, Miss.
   My ruler's broke in half.
   My ruler's broke in half.
   I've rubbed a hole in the paper.
   I've smudged mine with my scarf.
   Oh, oh, oh!

3. My work's blew out of the window, Miss.
   My work's fell in the bin.
   The leg's dropped off of my chair, Miss.
   And the ceiling's coming in.
   The ceiling's coming in.
   The leg's dropped off my chair.
   My work's fell in the bin.
   Oh, oh, oh!

4. I've ate a poison apple, Miss.
   I've held a poison pen.
   I think I'm being kidnapped, Miss.
   So . . . can we start again?

19 Headmaster's Hymn

Adapted from a Traditional Melody

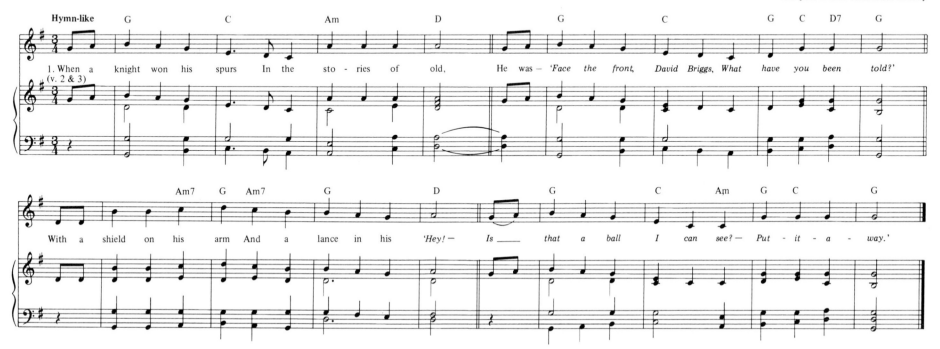

1. When a knight won his spurs
    In the stories of old,
    He was – 'Face the front, David Briggs,
    What have you been told?'
    With a shield on his arm
    And a lance in his – 'Hey! –
    Is that a ball I can see? –
    Put – it – a – way.'

2. No charger have I
    And – 'No talking back there. –
    You're supposed to be singing, –
    Not combing your hair.'
    Though back into storyland
    Giants have – 'Roy, –
    This isn't the playground, –
    Stop pushing that boy!'

3. Let faith be my shield
    And – 'Who's eating sweets here?
    I'm ashamed of you, Marion, –
    It's not like you dear.'
    And let me set free
    With – 'Please stop that, Paul King.
    This is no place for whistlers, –
    We'd rather you sing!'

Part Two  **HEARD IT IN**

THE PLAYGROUND

20 *The Mrs Butler Blues*

1. I've got the
   Teach-them-in-the-morning-
   Playground-duty-
   Teach-them-in-the-afternoon-blues.
   My head is like a drum;
   My feet are cold and sore.
   I'm feeling so glum;
   Can't take any more.
   Can't take any more!
   I've got the
   Teach-them-in-the-morning-
   Playground-duty-
   Teach-them-in-the-afternoon-blues.

2. I've got the
   Please-Miss-Tracey's-eating-
   Where's the-hamster?-
   Miss-I've-broke-my-ruler-blues.
   My hair is full of chalk.
   There's paint upon my dress.
   It hurts when I talk.
   My handbag's a mess.
   My handbag's a mess!
   I've got the
   Please-Miss-Tracey's-eating-
   Where's the-hamster?-
   Miss-I've-broke-my-ruler-blues.

3. I've got the
   Teach-them-till-I'm-weary-
   Parents'-evening-
   Didn't-get-home-till-midnight-blues.
   I know it's a job
   That has to be done,
   But I'd rather rob
   A bank with a gun.
   If you give me a gun!
   I've got the
   Teach-them-till-I'm-weary-
   Parents'-evening-
   Didn't-get-home-till-midnight-blues.

   Oh, teach-them-in-the-morning.
   Hmm!
   How'd you like to be in my . . . shoes?

21 Billy McBone

1. Billy McBone
   Had a mind of his own,
   Which he mostly kept under his hat.
   The teachers all thought
   That he could not be taught,
   But Bill didn't seem to mind that.
   Billy McBone
   Had a mind of his own,
   Which the teachers had searched for for years.
   Trying test after test,
   But they still never guessed
   It was hidden between his ears.

2. Billy McBone
   Had a mind of his own,
   Which only his friends ever saw.
   When the teacher said, 'Bill,
   Whereabouts is Brazil?'
   He just shuffled and stared at the floor.
   Billy McBone
   Had a mind of his own,
   Which he kept under lock and key.
   While the teachers in vain
   Tried to burgle his brain,
   His thoughts were off wandering free.

22 *The Ghost Teacher*

Slow and sad

1. The school is closed, the child-ren gone, But the ghost of a tea - cher lin-gers on.

As day-light fades, and day-time ends, As night draws in and dark des-cends, She stands in the class-room, as clear as glass, And calls out the names of her ab-sent class.

GLOCKENSPIEL and RECORDER

2. The school is shut, no child-ren there, But the ghost of the teach - er, un-a-ware, Puts the

Optional ending: Fade out gradually repeating *2 bars, and then go to the last two bars (*preferred* ending is as written here).

1. The school is closed, the children gone,
   But the ghost of a teacher lingers on.
   As daylight fades, and daytime ends,
   As night draws in and dark descends,
   She stands in the classroom, as clear as glass,
   And calls out the names of her absent class.

2. The school is shut, no children there,
   But the ghost of the teacher, unaware,
   Puts the date on the board and moves about
   (As night draws on and stars come out)
   Between the desks – a glow in the gloom –
   And calls for quiet in the silent room.

3. The school is a ruin, the children fled,
   But the ghost of the teacher, long-time dead,
   As the moon comes up and the first owls glide,
   Puts on her coat and steps outside.
   In the moonlit playground, shadow-free,
   She stands on duty with a cup of tea.

4. The school is forgotten – children forget –
   But the ghost of a teacher lingers yet.
   As night creeps up to the edge of day,
   She tidies the Plasticine away;
   Counts up the scissors – a shimmer of glass –
   And says, 'Off you go!' to her absent class.

   She utters the words that no one hears,
   Picks up her bag . . .

   and

   disappears.

23 The Old Teacher

*Suggested tambourine/woodblock rhythm omitting in stopped chord bars.

Latin American rhythm

f 1. There was an old teach-er __ Who lived in a school, __ Slept in the stock-cup-board __ as a rule, __ With

RECORDERS

sheets of __ white pa - per __ to make up __ her bed And a pil - low __ of hymn - books Un-der her head. __

2. There was an old teach-er ___ Who lived for years ___ In - side ___ a play - house, ___

RECORDERS

or so it ap-pears, ___ Eat - ing ___ the ap - ples ___ the child - ren ___ had brought her, And wash - ing ___ her face ___

In the gold - fish ___ wa - ter. 3. There was an old teach-er ___ Who end-ed her days ___ Watch-ing

schools' te-le-vi-sion — and child-ren's plays; Sav - ing — the strength she could just a - bout mus - ter, To pow - der — her

RECORDERS

nose _____ With the black - board dust - er.

molto rall. Slower

4. There was an old teach-er —

molto rall.

Faster (1st tempo)

Who fi - nal-ly died — Read-ing Ginn (Le-vel One), which she could not a - bide. The words on — her tomb - stone said: TEN OUT OF TEN,

And her grave, yes — her grave was — the sand - pit. — That's all — now. A - men.

f That's all — now. A - men.

1. There was an old teacher
   Who lived in a school,
   Slept in the stock-cupboard as a rule,
   With sheets of white paper to make up her bed
   And a pillow of hymn-books
   Under her head.

2. There was an old teacher
   Who lived for years
   Inside a play-house, or so it appears,
   Eating the apples the children had brought her,
   And washing her face
   In the goldfish water.

3. There was an old teacher
   Who ended her days
   Watching schools' television and children's plays;
   Saving the strength she could just about muster,
   To powder her nose
   With the blackboard duster.

4. There was an old teacher
   Who finally died
   Reading Ginn (Level One), which she could not abide.
   The words on her tombstone said: TEN OUT OF TEN,
   And her grave, yes her grave was the sand-pit.
   That's all now. Amen.

   That's all now. Amen.

24 Parents' Evening

1. We're wait-ing in the cor-ri-dor,__ My dad,__ my mum__ and me. They're sit-ting there and talk-ing;
(v. 2 & 3)

I'm ner-vous as can be. I won-der what she'll say to them.__ I'll say I've got a pain!

I wish I'd got my spell-ings right.__ I wish I had a brain. Who's go-ing to get the stick.

1. We're waiting in the corridor,
   My dad, my mum and me.
   They're sitting there and talking;
   I'm nervous as can be.
   I wonder what she'll say to them.
   I'll say I've got a pain!
   I wish I'd got my spellings right.
   I wish I had a brain.

2. We're waiting in the corridor,
   My husband, son and me.
   My son just stands there smiling;
   I'm smiling, nervously.
   I wonder what she'll say to us.
   I hope it's not *all* bad.
   He's such a good boy, really;
   But dozy – like his dad.

3. We're waiting in the corridor,
   My wife, my boy and me.
   My wife's as cool as cucumber;
   I'm nervous as can be.
   I hate these parents' evenings.
   The waiting makes me sick.
   I feel just like a kid again
   Who's going to get the stick.

4. I'm waiting in the classroom.
   It's nearly time to start.
   I wish there was a way to stop
   The pounding in my heart.
   The parents in the corridor
   Are chatting cheerfully;
   And now I've got to face them,
   And I'm nervous as can be.

25 *The Longest Kiss Contest*

1. We seen 'em in the cloakroom, Miss –
Ann Cram and Alan Owen;
Tryin' to have the longest kiss –
They had the stopwatch goin'!

   On your mouths,
   Get set – *go*!

2. And Alison – and Rose – and Chris!
They've been in there since playtime, Miss,
Tryin' to break the record,
They'll wear their lips away.

3. Ann 'n' Chris was winnin', Miss,
Till Dennis made them laugh.
He pulled a face, y'know – like this:
They're going to make a graph!

4. We seen 'em in the cloakroom, Miss –
Ann Cram and Alan Owen;
Tryin' to have the longest kiss –
They had the stopwatch goin'!

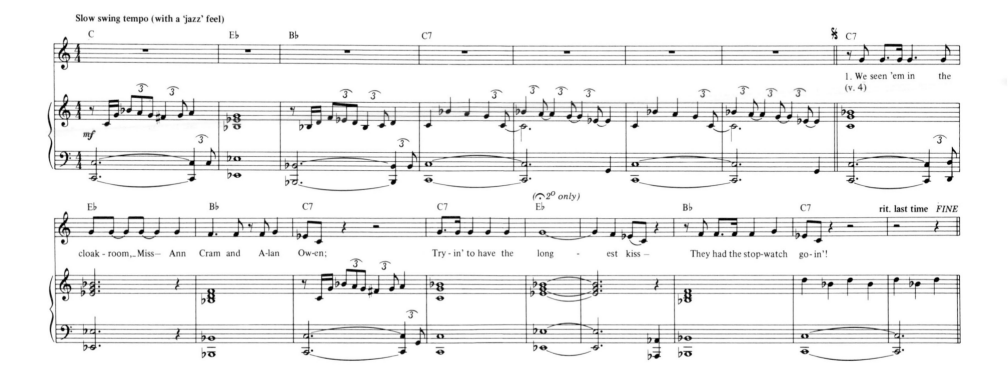

26 The Teacher's Prayer

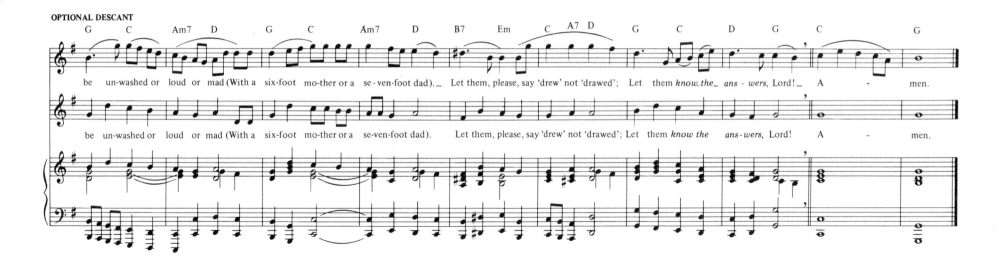

1. Let the children in our care
   Clean their shoes and comb their hair;
   Come to school on time – and neat,
   Blow their noses, wipe their feet.

2. Let them, Lord, *not* eat in class
   Or rush into the hall *en masse.*
   Let them show some self-control;
   Let them slow down; let them *stroll!*

3. Let the children in our charge
   Not be violent or large;
   Not be sick on the school-trip bus,
   Not be cleverer than us.

4. Not be unwashed or loud or mad
   (With a six-foot mother or a seven-foot dad).
   Let them, please, say 'drew' not 'drawed';
   Let them *know the answers*, Lord!

   Amen.

27 Finishing Off

1. Come here, Malcolm!
   Look at the state of your book.
   Stories and pictures unfinished
   Wherever I look.
   The model you started at Easter,
   The plaster casts of your feet,
   The graph of the local traffic –
   All of them incomplete.

2. Come here, Malcolm!
   Look at the state of your book.
   Stories and pictures unfinished
   Wherever I look.
   You've a half-baked pot in the kiln room
   And a half-eaten cake in your drawer.
   You don't even finish the jokes you tell –
   I really can't take any more.

3. Come here, Malcolm!
   Look at the state of your book.
   Stories and pictures unfinished
   Wherever I look.
   And Malcolm said . . . very little.
   He blinked and shuffled his feet.
   The sentence he finally started
   Remained incomplete.

4. He gazed for a time at the floorboards;
   He stared for a while into space;
   With an unlined, unwhiskered expression
   On his unfinished face.

28 I See a Seagull

1. I see a seagull in the playground.
   I see a crisp-bag and a glove;
   I see grey slides on the grey ice
   And a grey sky above.

2. I see a white bird in the playground
   And a pale face in the glass;
   A room reflected behind me,
   And the rest of the class.

3. I see a seagull in the playground.
   I see it fly away.
   I see a white bird in the grey sky:
   The lesson for today.

sea-gull   in the play-ground.__ I see a crisp-bag and a glove;__   I see grey slides__ on the grey ice__ And a grey__ sky_a-bove.__   2. I see a

white bird__   in the play-ground__ And a pale face__ in the glass;__   A room re-flect-ed__   be-hind me,   And the rest of__ the class.   3. I see a

sea-gull___ in the play-ground.___ I see it___ fly_ a - way.___ I see a white bird___ in the grey sky:___ The les-son_ for_____ to-day.

RECORDER I and GLOCK.

RECORDER II

VOICE

I see a

RECORDER I + GLOCK.

VOICE

sea-gull___ in the play-ground.___ I see a crisp-bag_ and_ a_ glove;___ I see grey slides___ on the grey-ice___ And a grey___ sky a-bove.

I see a white bird ____ in the play-ground ____ And a pale face ____ in the glass; ____ A room re - flect-ed ____ be-hind me, ____ And the rest of the

RECORDERS and GLOCK.

VOICE

class. 3. I see a sea - gull in the play-ground. ____ I see it ____ fly ____ a - way. ____ I see a white bird ____ in the grey sky: ____ The

RECORDER II

RECORDER I + GLOCK.

les - son ____ for ____ to - day.

29 Mrs So-and-so

Based on a Traditional Melody

Skipping

1. In the class-room Sits a tea-cher, Who she is we do not know. Our own tea-cher's Feel-ing poor-ly, We've got Mrs.__ So and so.
(vv. 2-5)

1. In the classroom
    Sits a teacher,
    Who she is we do not know.
    Our own teacher's
    Feeling poorly,
    We've got Mrs So-and-so.

2. Our own teacher's
    Firm but friendly,
    Lets us play out in the snow.
    Lets us dawdle
    In the cloakroom,
    Not like Mrs So-and-so.

3. Stop that pushing!
    Stop that shoving!
    Line up quietly in a row.
    Somehow life
    Is not the same with
    Bossy Mrs So-and-so.

4. Our own teacher's
    Kind and clever –
    Not a lot she doesn't know.
    Where's the pencils?
    What's your name, dear?
    Says this Mrs So-and-so.

5. Now at last
    Our teacher's better
    And it's time for *her* to go.
    Funny thing is
    Somehow we've got . . .
    Used to Mrs So-and-so.

30 The Grumpy Teacher

Sea shanty ('What shall we do with the drunken sailor')

1. 4. What shall we do with the grum-py tea-cher? What shall we do with the grum-py tea-cher? What shall we do with the grum-py tea-cher? Ear-ly in the morn-ing? 2. 5. Hang her on a hook be-hind the class-room door.—

Tie her up and leave her in the P. E. store.— Make her be with De-rek Drew for ev-er more,— Ear-ly in the morn-ing. 3. 6. Please, Miss, we're on-ly jok-ing, Don't mean to be pro-vok-ing.

How come your ears are smo-king? Ear-ly in the morn-ing. 7. What shall we do with the grum-py tea-cher? What shall we do with the grum-py tea-cher? What shall we do with the grum-py tea-cher,

Ear-ly in the morn-ing? 8. Tick-le her toes with a hair-y crea-ture. Leave her in the jun-gle where the ants can reach her. BRING HER BACK A-LIVE TO BE A CLASS-ROOM TEA-CHER! Ear - ly— in the—morn-ing!

1. What shall we do with the grumpy teacher?
    What shall we do with the grumpy teacher?
    What shall we do with the grumpy teacher,
    Early in the morning?

2. Hang her on a hook behind the classroom door.
    Tie her up and leave her in the P. E. store.
    Make her be with Derek Drew for evermore,
    Early in the morning.

3. Please, Miss, we're only joking,
    Don't mean to be provoking.
    How come your ears are smoking?
    Early in the morning.

4. What shall we do with the grumpy teacher?
    What shall we do with the grumpy teacher?
    What shall we do with the grumpy teacher,
    Early in the morning?

5. Send him out to duty when the sleet is sleeting.
    Keep him after school to take a parents' meeting.
    Stand him in the hall to watch the children eating,
    Early in the morning.

6. Please, Sir, we're only teasing.
    Don't mean to be displeasing.
    Help – that's our necks you're squeezing!
    Early in the morning.

7. What shall we do with the grumpy teacher?
    What shall we do with the grumpy teacher?
    What shall we do with the grumpy teacher,
    Early in the morning?

8. Tickle her toes with a hairy creature.
    Leave her in the jungle where the ants can reach her.
    BRING HER BACK ALIVE TO BE A CLASSROOM TEACHER!
    Early – in the – morning!

31 Leavers' Song

Based on a traditional melody

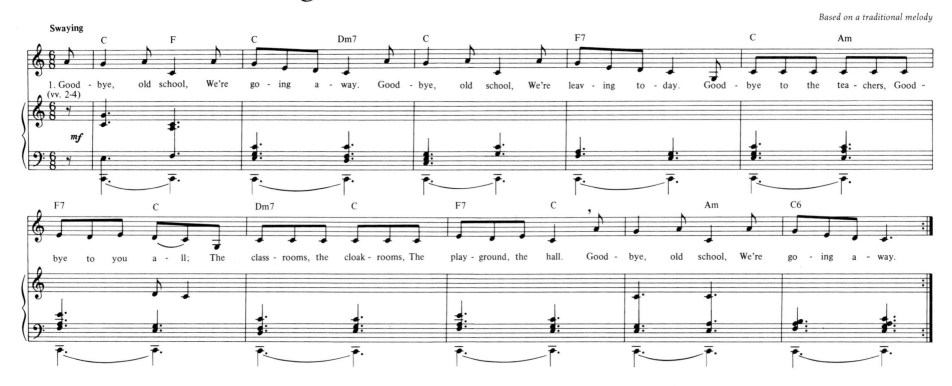

1. Goodbye, old school,
   We're going away.
   Goodbye, old school,
   We're leaving today.
   Goodbye to the teachers,
   Goodbye to you all;
   The classrooms, the cloakrooms,
   The playground, the hall.
   Goodbye, old school,
   We're going away.

2. Goodbye, old school,
   We'll miss you a lot –
   The din and the dinners,
   Believe it or not.
   We'll miss you, Miss,
   And remember you, Sir,
   When lessons have faded
   And homework's a blur.
   Goodbye, old school,
   We'll miss you a lot.

3. Goodbye, old school,
   We'll never forget
   The smell of the cloakrooms
   With coats soaking wet.
   The balls on the roof
   And the songs on the bus.
   We'll think of you –
   Will you think of us?
   Goodbye, old school,
   We'll never forget.

4. Goodbye, old school,
   What more can we say?
   It's *bon voyage*,
   It's anchors aweigh.
   The desks are quite empty;
   The classroom is bare;
   But our hearts are full
   And you'll always be there.
   Goodbye, old school,
   What more can we say?

Part Three  **FOUR MORE**

32 Night School

1. Good - night, dear dad-dy, __ Good-night, dear pa, We're off to the Night School, __

We're go-ing — hurr-ah! 2. Sleep well, dear mum-my, __ Sleep well, dear ma, We'll be back in the morn-ing, __

Till then — ta - ra! 3. With our bed-time books and our ted-dy__ bears, In nigh-ties and py-ja-mas we de-scend the stairs, __ Step out-side on__ slip-pered feet__ And

1. Goodnight, dear daddy,
Goodnight, dear pa,
We're off to the Night School,
We're going – hurrah!

2. Sleep well, dear mummy,
Sleep well, dear ma,
We'll be back in the morning,
Till then – tara!

3. With our bedtime books and our teddy
bears,
In nighties and pyjamas we descend the
stairs,
Step outside on slippered feet
And hurry down the lamp-lit street,
Hurry through the Night School gate
Right on time, though the time is late.

4. Doze off, dear mummy,
And snuggle down.
Our teacher's arrived
In his dressing-gown.

5. Sleep tight, dear daddy,
And softly snore.
Our lessons have started:
What's nine times four?

6. But it's not just sums, we're pleased to
say,
That rapidly pass the night away,
For the clock ticks on and pretty soon
We're out to play by the light of the
moon.
Then, while the stars shine in the east,
It's into the hall for a midnight feast.

7. Sweet dreams, dear mummy,
We're eating pies
While golden slumbers
Fill your eyes.

8. Doze on, dear daddy,
At mummy's side.
In the midnight oil
Our chips are fried.

9. Well it's home time now, the day is dawning,
The hamster is asleep and the teacher's yawning.
We leave the Night School on slippered feet
And dawdle on down the misty street
With our bedtime books and teddy bears
In nighties and pyjamas we ascend the stairs.

10. Good morning, daddy,
Our eyes are lead.
We're terribly dozy
And . . . (yawn) . . . ready for bed.

11. Good morning, mummy,
Good morning, ma.
We'll sleep all day
And see you . . . Ah! (yawn).

33 Scatterbrain

Bouncing

1. My writ-ing's gone all crook-ed_ My writ-ing's gone all small (v.2) My

writ-ing's gone all squashed up Like it ran in-to a wall, Ran in-to a wall._ My maths has gone all hay-wire_ I need some ans-wers quick. My book is full of kiss-es And there's

not a sin-gle tick, Not a sin-gle tick. My 3. din-ner's gone all slud-gy_ The chips are_ look-ing wierd. The gra-vy's tak-ing ov-er And the

Much slower

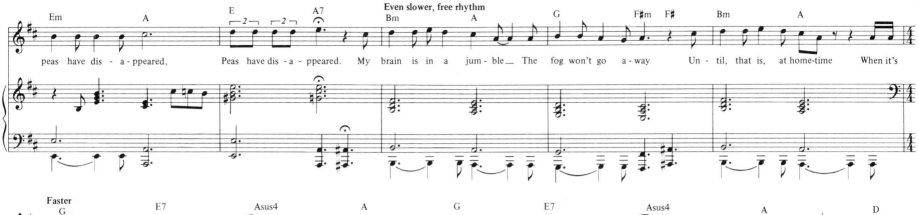

peas have dis - a - ppeared,   Peas have dis - a - ppeared.   My brain is in a   jum - ble___ The   fog won't go a - way   Un - til, that is, at home-time   When it's

all...   *as clear as___ day.* ___   All as clear as___ day ___   Hur - ray!

ff (with fist)

1. My writing's gone all crooked
   My writing's gone all small
   My writing's gone all squashed up
   Like it ran into a wall,
   Ran into a wall.
   My maths has gone all haywire
   I need some answers quick.
   My book is full of kisses
   And there's not a single tick,
   Not a single tick.

2. My painting's gone all smudgy
   My painting's gone all wet.
   The sky's run down the hillside
   And the cow should see a vet,
   Cow should see a vet.
   My model's gone all wobbly
   I think I need more glue.
   The only bit that's sticking's
   On the bottom of my shoe,
   Bottom of my shoe.

3. My dinner's gone all sludgy
   The chips are looking weird.
   The gravy's taking over
   And the peas have disappeared,
   Peas have disappeared.
   My brain is in a jumble
   The fog won't go away
   Until, that is, at home time
   When it's all . . . *as clear as day,*
   All as clear as day.

   Hurray!

34 Everybody Was a Baby Once

1. Everybody was a baby once.
   Everybody was a baby once.
   Everybody went to beddy
   With a little furry teddy.
   Everybody was a baby once.

2. Oh, your daddy was a baby once.
   And your mummy was a baby once.
   Yes, your daddy and your mummy
   Used to sit and suck a dummy.
   Everybody was a baby once.

3. The baby comes first in life's great
   plan;
   Everyone started out small.
   The child is father to the man;
   The race begins at a crawl.

4. Oh, your grandad was a baby once,
   And your granny was a baby once.
   Yes, your granny – please don't laugh –
   Used to widdle in the bath.
   Everybody was a baby once.

5. Oh, your teacher was a baby once.
   Yes, your teacher was a baby once.
   She would scream and bawl and shout,
   And she'd spit her dinner out –
   Everybody was a baby once.

6. Life begins with a baby's cry;
   Life begins in a cot.
   A little tear in a little eye;
   A little bum on a pot.
   A little bum on a pot.

7. Oh, you and you were all babies once,
   You and you were all babies once.
   Yes, you and you were happy
   Just to sit and fill a nappy.
   Everybody was a baby once.

8. Everybody was a baby once.
   Everybody was a baby once.
   Everybody was a baby –
   Even Mrs Thatcher*, maybe!
   Everybody was a baby once.

* Long-serving British prime minister (late twentieth century). You can always substitute this with the name of your teacher/headteacher!

35 *A Happy School*

Stately, flowing

1. There was a hap-py school __ Long, long a - go, High on a

moun-tain top __ Lost in the snow. Oh, how __ the child - ren __ ran When they saw the

chest - nut man Cook-ing hot che - est-nuts in his pan Long, long a - go.

Verse 3

3. There is a hap-py school ___ Up in the sky, Wait - ing for all of us ___ To come by-and - by.

Oh, how ___ the an - gels yell When they hear the din - ner bell.

Some-thing is cook-ing, they can tell, Up in the sky.

1. There was a happy school
   Long, long ago,
   High on a mountain top
   Lost in the snow.
   Oh, how the children ran
   When they saw the chestnut man
   Cooking hot chestnuts in his pan
   Long, long ago.

2. There is a happy school
   Far, far away,
   Where they have strawberry pie
   Three times a day.
   Oh, how the children shout
   When the teachers serve it out.
   There will be seconds, too, have no doubt,
   Far, far away.

3. There is a happy school
   Up in the sky,
   Waiting for all of us
   To come by-and-by.
   Oh, how the angels yell
   When they hear the dinner bell.
   Something is cooking, they can tell,
   Up in the sky.